The Magic of Disney

STORYBOOK COLLECTION

Disney PRESS

New York

TABLE OF CONTENTS

TABLE OF CONTENTS

Designed by Alfred Giuliani

First Edition

10 9 8 7 6 5 4 3 2

This book is set in 20-point Cochin.

Library of Congress Catalog Card Number: 2004103807

ISBN 0-7868-3523-0

For more Disney Press fun, visit www.disneybooks.com

Walt Disney's

The Big
Bear Scare

"It's a beautiful day to go camping!" Mickey Mouse exclaimed to his nephews and Goofy as he locked

the front door of his house. "Are you sure we have everything?"

"We're all ready to go, Uncle Mickey!" cried Morty.

"Ferdie and I packed all the pots and pans and stuff we could possibly need."

"We've been ready to leave since daybreak!" added Ferdie excitedly.

"And *I've* packed enough food in my backpack for three days, Mickey!" Goofy said. "At first, I couldn't get it all in, but I finally found room for everything."

Mickey smiled. "That's great!" he cried. "And the tent's ready to be put up as soon as we get to our campsite. I'm glad we've all planned so carefully for this trip."

"Uncle Mickey, let's follow the new bike trail out to the lake," Ferdie suggested.

"Okay, boys," Mickey agreed. "That's a good idea."

The hike began well. Sunshine warmed the breeze, and the birds sang happy songs. After a while, the friends stopped to snack on some blackberries that 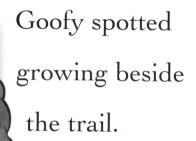 Goofy spotted growing beside the trail.

"I think this will be the best campout we've ever had," Mickey told his friends.

As Goofy turned around to agree, he tripped over a log and sprawled out on the ground. His bulging backpack came open, and

everything in it tumbled out onto the grass.

"Oh, no!" Goofy groaned. "You fellows go on and find a good campsite. I'll repack this stuff and catch up as soon as I can."

"Okay, Goofy. We'll have everything set up for supper when you get there with the food," Mickey said.

"See you later!" the nephews called back from the trail.

While Goofy scrambled to put his pack together again, someone just out of sight watched with quiet interest.

A hungry mother bear had come to visit her favorite berry patch. She stood behind a bush, only a few feet

away from Goofy. Then, when his back was turned, she snatched the largest package off the ground, and disappeared into the brush.

A few minutes later, Goofy hurried to catch up with his friends, scratching his head in bewilderment. "This time, everything fits into my backpack just right," he mumbled. "I wonder why."

"Hi, Goofy!" Mickey cried, greeting his friend at the campsite. "Why don't you start supper while I finish setting up the tent? I'm almost done."

"We've already unpacked the pots and pans, Goofy. We'll help you!" said Morty and Ferdie eagerly.

"Mountain air really makes you hungry, doesn't it, boys?" said Goofy. "We'll have fish tomorrow, but tonight we'll have the steaks I brought in my pack!"

Thinking how good the steaks would taste, Goofy hurriedly opened his backpack. "Here are the marshmallows—and the bread—and the peanut butter—and the pancake mix. And here—" He stopped suddenly. "The steaks! The steaks are gone!"

"They can't be!"
Mickey exclaimed.

"I must have left
them at the place
where my back-
pack fell open,"
explained Goofy.

"Well," Mickey
said, "that's not so

bad. We'll just follow the trail back there and get them.

Come on! Let's hurry!"

The four campers ran down the trail. When they came to the berry bushes, however, the missing steaks were nowhere to be found.

"I've spoiled the best camping trip ever," Goofy said sadly. "How could I have lost them?" He could not be comforted, no matter what anyone said to him.

Meanwhile, at the camp, three uninvited guests had arrived. The mother bear and her two cubs had come to visit.

The cubs quickly discovered that banging pots and pans together was fun. Their mother decided that the tent made a great den, and she settled down comfortably inside it.

"What's that racket?" Mickey wondered as they returned to their camp. Cautiously, they hid in the brush nearby and peered into the clearing.

"Oh, no! Bear cubs!" Ferdie moaned.

"Shh!" warned Mickey. "Maybe they'll leave soon.

But isn't it funny that they haven't eaten the other food yet?"

Suddenly, Morty realized what had happened to their steaks. "I'll bet they aren't hungry!" he cried. "*They're* the ones who ate our steaks!"

"Uncle Mickey!" Ferdie whispered. "Look! Something's moving inside our tent!"

"Grrrrr," rumbled the mother bear softly as she turned over to lie on her other side.

"It must be the cubs' mother!" Mickey cried worriedly. "How will we ever get her out of there?"

I have to do
something,
Goofy thought.
Otherwise, our
whole trip will
be spoiled—and
it will be my
fault. He looked
around and
noticed a pail of

water standing near the firewood. It gave him an idea.

While Mickey and the boys watched anxiously, Goofy crawled out of the brush, straight to the pail of water. He had never moved so quietly and carefully in all his life. Grasping the pail, he slowly inched his way back into the brush.

Now, Goofy thought as he hid behind a large tree trunk, I'll climb this tree and dump the water on the bears. A shower should scare them away!

However, the cubs had seen the pail disappear into the brush and were watching for it to reappear. Soon they saw the pail moving slowly and jerkily up the side of the tree trunk!

"Here comes the mother bear!" Mickey warned. "She wants to see why the cubs are so quiet."

Climbing the tree was more difficult than Goofy had imagined. I must be high enough now, he thought as he reached for an overhead tree limb. He peeked around the trunk and prepared to take aim. And what did he see? He saw all three bears—staring right at *him*!

At the same moment the tree limb cracked. "HELP!" cried Goofy.

Crash! Splash! Leaves, tree limb, branches, pail, water, and Goofy all plunged down, flattening the tent!

Startled, the mother bear decided that she and her cubs had seen enough. They ran off, disappearing into the thick woods.

"The bears have left! The bears have left!" all four campers cheered with relief.

Safe beside the campfire that evening, Morty said, "We've had an exciting day!"

"Goofy found just the right way to send the bears home," said Mickey. "He saved the whole trip!"

"Aww, it wasn't anything," Goofy said shyly. But he was grinning from ear to ear.

Walt Disney's

Some Ducks
Have All the Luck

For Daisy

It was a warm summer day, but Donald Duck was not outside enjoying the beautiful sunny weather. Instead, he was inside his house, pacing. He was very upset.

"Unca Donald, are you feeling okay?" asked Huey.

"What's wrong?" asked Dewey.

"Stop pacing! You're making us dizzy!" cried Louie.

"Today is Daisy's birthday," declared Donald, "and I need to get her a better present than that Gladstone Gander does. But I'm not quite sure what to buy her."

"That's easy, Unca Donald," said Huey.

"Just get Daisy a bigger, fancier present than Gladstone Gander does," said Dewey.

"But Gladstone's so lucky, and I have the worst luck. Also, I'm broke," Donald

complained. "He will probably buy Daisy something really expensive. And besides, how can I buy something better when I don't even know what he's giving her?"

Just then, Donald glanced out the window and noticed someone walking down the street.

"It's Gladstone Gander!" he exclaimed. "Maybe it's my lucky day after all. I'll follow him all over town until I see what he's buying for Daisy."

Meanwhile, Gladstone Gander was also worrying about Daisy's gift.

I sure hope I am lucky today, he thought as he walked down the street. I have to come up with a really great present for Daisy's birthday.

"Ah, this must be my good luck now!" Gladstone exclaimed when he saw some money lying on the

sidewalk. But it was only a one-dollar bill. "Every little bit helps," Gladstone said with a sigh as he put the bill in his pocket. Poor Donald

groaned as he watched Gladstone put the money away. Some ducks have all the luck, thought Donald.

As he started walking again, Gladstone Gander had a funny feeling. I think I'm being followed, he thought.

Gladstone stopped at a jewelry store and pretended to look in the window. He wanted to know who was following him.

He chuckled when he recognized Donald Duck's reflection in the store window.

I bet Donald is as worried about Daisy's present as I am, thought Gladstone. I know just how to give him a real scare!

Gladstone Gander marched into the jewelry store and looked around. He soon spotted some sparkly diamond bracelets. He held one up, making sure that Donald Duck saw. He wanted Donald to think he was going to give Daisy a diamond bracelet for her birthday.

Outside, poor Donald Duck groaned again. That must have been a thousand-dollar bill he had found!

Now he's buying Daisy a diamond bracelet. Some ducks have all the luck, Donald thought.

Gladstone's next stop was the Bonbon Boutique, which sold the most expensive and most delicious chocolates in Duckburg. And it happened to be one of Daisy's favorite stores.

Donald went into the store after Gladstone came
out. He almost fainted when the clerk told him the

price of one

14-karat

chocolate

bonbon.

Donald

caught up

with

Gladstone

Gander outside the Sniff of Success Perfume Shop.

Gladstone couldn't resist teasing Donald.

"Fancy meeting you here, Donald. I was just trying to decide what to give Daisy for her birthday—a diamond bracelet, a 14-karat chocolate bonbon, or a bottle of Liquid Gold: The Perfume Too Expensive to Wear," said Gladstone gleefully.

Donald slunk away.

I guess this wasn't my lucky day, after all, he thought. I never should have followed Gladstone. He has all the luck.

Gladstone Gander laughed as Donald walked away.

But soon he remembered that he still had no present for Daisy and only one dollar in his pocket.

I need some good luck, and I need it now, thought Gladstone as he hurried home.

"Hello, Mr. Gander," said the mail carrier. "I just left a special-delivery letter in your mailbox."

"Maybe I've won another contest," Gladstone said as he tore open the envelope. He read eagerly, "'You have

been selected to receive a free dinner for two at the grand opening of Chez Swann, the swankiest restaurant in Duckburg.'"

Gladstone whooped. "My good luck strikes again! This is the perfect present for Daisy. Donald doesn't have a chance."

Meanwhile, Donald Duck was sadly climbing the

steps of his

house.

"We

have a big

surprise for

you, Unca

Donald,"

said Huey,

Dewey,

and Louie.

"I'm not interested in surprises," Donald said with a groan.

"But we found out what Aunt Daisy wants most for her birthday, and we got it for you to give to her," said Huey.

"The present is all wrapped up and waiting in the car," added Louie.

"So, let's go!" shouted Dewey, racing for the car.

Donald and his nephews had been at Daisy's house

for a little while when there was a knock at the door. It was Gladstone Gander.

"Happy birthday, dear Daisy!" Gladstone exclaimed. "How would you like to go to the opening night of Chez Swann, the swankiest restaurant in Duckburg?"

"I'd love to go, Gladstone," Daisy replied. "But I simply can't leave my darling kitty cat that Donald just gave me." Daisy petted the tiny kitten. It purred and purred and purred.

"But I have a wonderful idea!"

Daisy cried. "Why don't you and Donald have my

birthday dinner together? You can go to Chez Swann and sing 'Happy Birthday' to me." Then Daisy showed them both to the door.

Donald Duck had a great time at Chez Swann. He lifted his glass and toasted, "To Daisy!"

"To Daisy," Gladstone Gander agreed. Then he grumbled, "Some ducks have all the luck."

Walt Disney's

Mickey Mouse
and the
Pet Shop

Mr. Palmer, who owned the local pet shop, was going on an overnight trip. He couldn't leave the animals by themselves, so he asked his good friend

NOT FOR SALE

Mickey Mouse to watch the shop while he was gone. He gave Mickey a full set of instructions on how to take care of the animals.

"I will be back tomorrow afternoon," said Mr. Palmer as he waved good-bye. "You shouldn't have any problems."

"Have a good time," called Mickey. "This will be a snap!"

"A snap!" repeated Mr. Palmer's pet parrot.

Once Mr. Palmer had gone, Mickey quickly settled

in. He decided he wanted to get to know all the animals

he would be taking care of. So he walked around,

gazing at the
colorful fish,
talking parrots,
furry kittens,
and cuddly
dogs. All the
animals seemed
content—all but

one, that is. A cute little puppy was whining and whimpering in the saddest way.

"Poor little fella," said Mickey. "What you need is some attention."

Mickey lifted the puppy from the kennel. "Steady, boy," said Mickey. But the lively puppy was anxious to be out and wriggled himself free from Mickey's arms. He then raced over to the goldfish bowl for a drink of water.

"Watch out!" screeched the parrot. "Watch out!"

But it was too late. The puppy knocked over the

bowl. *Crash*—it fell to the floor and broke into a

million

pieces.

And the

poor fish

went

flying

across the

room.

"Gotcha!" Mickey called as he caught the fish. He then put it in a new fishbowl.

"Crash! Crash!" squawked the parrot, furiously flapping its wings.

This was not a good start to the day, thought Mickey.

Mickey decided that the best thing to do was to put the puppy back in the kennel. "Now, you can't cause any more trouble," he said.

Just then, he heard the door open. It was his first customer of the day, and Mickey was excited. So excited that he forgot to lock the kennel door.

"Can I help you?" Mickey asked.

But before the customer could answer, the puppy

got free and opened a cage that held four mice. The

mice ran out

and raced

around the

store.

"Eeek! I'll

come back

later. Much

later!" cried the customer as she ran out the door.

After she had gone, Mickey gathered up all the pets and put them back where they belonged. This time, he made sure he locked the kennel door.

"Don't

worry,

little guy,"

he said

to the

puppy.

"Someone

will buy you. You'll see."

That night Mickey stayed in the bedroom above the pet shop. As he tried to sleep, the puppy howled at the top of his lungs. Mickey tried hiding under the covers.

But that didn't work. Then he tried covering his ears with a pillow, but that didn't work, either. Mickey didn't know what to do.

Finally, the puppy got exactly what he wanted—a cozy spot under the covers, right next to Mickey!

When Mickey woke up the next morning, the puppy was gone. Mickey looked all over the house for him, but he was nowhere to be found. Maybe he is down in the pet shop, thought Mickey. Mickey went downstairs to check.

When he walked into the store, he couldn't believe his eyes. The place was a mess! Books were scattered all over the floor, and one of the plants had been turned over. Worse, he still couldn't find the puppy anywhere!

Mickey got dressed and then began searching high and low for his little friend. After looking through the entire store, Mickey was about to give up. But he decided to check the storage room just in case the little puppy had found his way in there. Sure enough, he

caught sight of a wriggling bundle of fish food. The puppy was inside the bag.

Mickey picked up the puppy and brought him back to the kennel and locked the door. "Now you can't cause any more trouble," he said.

"Well," Mickey added with a sigh, "I guess I should begin tidying up the store."

As he worked, Mickey heard the little puppy barking from the kennel. Mickey felt bad for the puppy, so he let him out again. This time the puppy was helpful. He helped Mickey put the books back on the shelf. He helped Mickey dust the counter. And he helped Mickey sweep up the dirt.

"You may be a rascal," said Mickey, "but I sure am getting used to having you around."

When they finished cleaning up, Mickey put the puppy back in the kennel. Then Mr. Palmer strode in. "It looks like everything went smoothly," he said. "I hope none of the animals gave you any trouble."

"It was as easy as pie," replied a very tired Mickey.

Then Mr. Palmer handed Mickey his paycheck. "Thanks for helping me out," he said. "I hope you'll come back soon."

Mickey just smiled.

As Mickey was about to leave, the puppy began to howl and scratch at the door of the kennel.

"I'm going to miss you, too, little fella," said Mickey sadly.

Suddenly,
Mickey had
a great idea:
he'd take the
pup instead of
the pay! Now,
everybody was
very happy—

especially the parrot, who screeched, "And don't come

back!"

"But what should I call you?" Mickey asked the puppy.

Just then, he saw a newspaper headline: NEW PICTURES OF PLANET PLUTO!

"That's it! I'll call you Pluto!" exclaimed Mickey.

Pluto gave his new master a big wet kiss, and from that day on, Mickey and Pluto were the best of friends.

DISNEY's
SPORT GOOFY
AND THE RACING ROBOT

It was race day, and the crowd was on their feet, clapping and cheering! The news photographers were quickly snapping pictures.

With a late burst of speed, Sport Goofy ran to the finish line. He had won the race!

"What a great athlete Sport Goofy is!" shouted a fan.

"He runs like the wind!" exclaimed another.

But there was one spectator who hadn't come to cheer for Sport Goofy. His name was Big Bad Pete—

and he was a crook. Pete watched while the mayor awarded Sport Goofy a trophy.

Then the mayor handed Sport Goofy a check for a great deal of money.

"That's the last prize money Sport Goofy is going to win," Pete muttered to himself. "Next time, I'll be the one who will collect the check!" With that, Pete stomped away.

The mayor wanted to make a long speech, but Sport Goofy quickly excused himself. "I have some errands to run," he said to the mayor, and he went on his way.

First, Sport Goofy ran to the bank, where he cashed his check. Next, he dashed into a sporting-goods store, where he bought racquets, bats, balls, and other sports equipment. After that, he raced all the way across town.

He stopped running when he arrived at the orphanage. "Look what I have for you," he said to the boys
and girls as he handed out the equipment.

The children's eyes always brightened with joy when

Sport

Goofy

came to

visit them.

He was

their best

friend.

Each and every child thanked Sport Goofy for the equipment. The director of the orphanage also thanked him.

"There's another race next week," Sport Goofy told them. "If I win the prize money again, I'm going to buy  that field over there for you children. Then you'll have lots of room to run and play!"

In the meantime, Big Bad Pete was planning something very dishonest. He was putting together a robot. When it was completed, Pete was going to enter it in the race against Sport Goofy.

"My robot will look so much like a real person," snarled Pete to himself, "that it will fool everyone!"

A week later, the runners arrived at the track. Once again, crowds of people came to watch Sport Goofy run. Everyone was so glad to see him that they didn't

pay any attention to the new runner that Pete had entered in the race.

"His name is Zippy," Pete told the entry judge.

While the runners were lining up to begin the race, Pete hid behind a nearby fence. He wanted to be sure no one saw him pressing the buttons on the remote control that would make his robot run.

The starter gave the signal and —*whoosh!*—the athletes were off and running.

Sport Goofy had a determined look on his face. He was thinking of

the children in the orphanage. I have to win this race so I can buy that playing field for them, he thought.

Looking out from his hiding place, Pete began to worry. Sport Goofy was running farther ahead of Zippy the Robot with every step.

Before long, the runners were nearing the finish line. "No, you don't, Sport Goofy!" growled Pete. He pressed the EXTRA FAST button on his remote control and —*zoom!*— Zippy streaked ahead and won the race.

Sport Goofy felt sad. Losing the race meant he would not be able to buy the playing field for the

children at the orphanage. Still, he congratulated the winner, for he was always a good sport.

The mayor also shook hands with Zippy and said, "Here's your trophy. And here's your check."

At that very instant, Pete appeared and quickly snatched the check from the mayor's hand. "I'll take that," he growled. "I'm his manager!" There was a reason why Pete was in a hurry. He had made his flimsy robot run extra fast, and now he was afraid it would begin to fall apart.

Grabbing hold of Zippy's hand, Pete started to run.

Suddenly, puffs of smoke came out of the robot's ears.

A spring inside the robot snapped, and —*ping!*—its head flew off! Everybody gasped in surprise.

"That isn't a PERSON," said the mayor. "It's a ROBOT!"

As Zippy
continued
to fall apart,
Pete let go
of him and

tried to flee with the trophy and check.

The mayor
stepped in front of
him. "Oh, no, you
don't, you
scoundrel!" he cried.

"Robots don't belong in races with PEOPLE,"

continued the mayor. "That's cheating."

The mayor took the trophy and check from Big Bad Pete and gave them both to Sport Goofy. "You are the rightful winner," he declared.

"Whenever I cheat, I get caught!" Pete grumbled as he kicked the dirt.

The day after the race, Sport Goofy kept his promise.

He bought the playing field with his prize money.

"The boys and girls will get a lot of good exercise now," said Sport Goofy to the director of the orphanage.

The director nodded his head in agreement. "You are truly the best friend a child could ever have, Sport Goofy!" he said.

Walt Disney's
Donald Duck Cleans Up

Donald Duck was in his backyard, taking a nap in his hammock, when he suddenly heard someone yell, "Donald Duck! Wake up!"

Sure enough, the sharp, scolding voice awoke Donald from a lovely dream he was having. Startled, he sat up in the hammock and looked at his neighbors, who had

gathered around him. They were all staring at Donald, and they did not look very happy.

"Wh-what's going on here?" Donald asked them. "Is something wrong?"

"There certainly is something wrong," said the lady who lived next door. "Donald Duck, this is Clean-Up Week, and we've all been busy for days painting our houses to make them look nice. Now, we want to know

when you plan to fix up *your* house. It's the worst-looking place on the block."

"Oh, it's not so bad," Donald said, looking at the chipped and peeling paint on his house. "I'll tend to it some day. But right now I'm in the middle of taking a nap."

"Oh, no, you don't, Donald Duck!" snapped the lady, pointing her finger at him. "You'll paint your house *today*. Or else you will have all of us to deal with."

All the neighbors looked at Donald angrily. He didn't want everyone to be upset with him, so he said, "Okay. I will get to it right away."

Then Donald's neighbors started to walk back to their homes, muttering and shaking their heads.

After his neighbors had left, Donald lay back in his

hammock with a deep frown. Even though he had told

his neighbors that he would paint his house, he really

didn't want to. But unless he thought of something

right away,

he would

have several

hours of

hard work

ahead of

him.

"What's the matter, Donald? Are you hurt?" asked two little chipmunks. Donald looked up and saw Chip 'n' Dale looking down at him from a maple branch. Suddenly, he had a wonderful idea.

"That's right, boys," he said with a groan. "I just fell down and twisted my leg. And the neighbors say I have to paint my house this very day—or else!"

"Say, that's too bad," the little chipmunks said sadly.

"I don't suppose you fellas could help me out?" Donald asked slyly.

"Do you mean help paint?" wondered Chip.

"Us?" asked Dale.

"That's right," said Donald. "It's really lots of fun. I wish I could do it myself, but I can't."

"Well—" said the chipmunks doubtfully. But they were too late.

Donald, who was limping slightly, was already pushing them toward the garage. "The paint's in there," he said. "And the brushes are on the shelf. Thanks a lot for helping me out, fellas."

As soon as Chip 'n' Dale had gone into the garage, Donald had a good laugh. "What a smart duck I am!" he said to himself. "My house will be painted, and I won't have to do a single thing!"

Chip 'n' Dale had never painted a house before, and they hardly knew where to begin. But inside the garage they found the paint they needed, and together, with all their might, they dragged the paint pails outside.

The brushes were too heavy for them to use, so they dipped their bushy tails into the paint instead. Back and forth they ran around the house, painting with their tails. They changed the house from a dingy gray to a bright, sunny yellow.

A few hours later, the house was finally all painted. Chip 'n' Dale were both exhausted.

"Whee-ew! This is hard work!" exclaimed Chip. "I've rubbed all the fur off my beautiful tail."

"Me, too," said Dale. "But poor Donald really needed our help. Let's go tell him we're all finished."

Wearily, the two little chipmunks trudged around the house. They were excited to show Donald what a good job they had done. However, when they reached the backyard, they could hardly believe their eyes.

The hammock was empty!

They looked around, but Donald Duck was nowhere

to be found.

"Why—

he—he's gone!"

exclaimed Chip.

"Wait!

Look over

there!" yelled

Dale. "There

he is, skipping

down the street. We've been tricked!"

At first, the chipmunks were too angry to do anything. They couldn't quite believe that Donald Duck had fooled them. They sat quietly for a few moments. Suddenly, the two chipmunks looked at one another. They had the perfect idea. "Back to the paint!" they called to each other as they quickly scampered to the garage.

"Red paint, white paint, purple paint, and green paint," Chip called, pointing at the shelf.

"We'll fix that smart duck!" snapped Dale.

And they did. For the next hour, they painted faster than ever before. When they had finished, they had . . .

painted the porch rails in bright red and white stripes . . .

painted purple scallops around every window . . .

painted a different pattern on every shutter . . .

painted a big, funny face on Donald Duck's front door . . .

and last, but not least, painted pink

and yellow polka dots on the roof.

If you had happened to pass Donald Duck's house that evening, you would have seen a very strange sight. All the neighbors were gathered in a circle in front of the house. They looked very angry. In the center of the circle stood Donald Duck.

He had a paintbrush in his hand, and he was holding

a bucket of paint.

"And what's more," the lady next door said, "we're

going to stay right here until you've cleaned up every

bit of this mess, Donald Duck. Now, get busy!"

"That's right, get busy," echoed two little voices. And if you had happened to look up at that very moment, you would have seen two little chipmunks chuckling to themselves high up in the maple tree.

Walt Disney's
Mickey Mouse
and the
KITTEN-SITTERS

"Guess what?" said Mickey Mouse to his nephews, Morty and Ferdie. "We're going to be kitten-sitters. Minnie is leaving her kitten, Figaro, with us tonight while she visits her Cousin Millie."

At that moment, there was wild clucking, flapping, and crowing coming from next door. Suddenly, Pluto the pup came racing across the lawn, with a big, angry rooster close behind him.

Pluto hid under the porch while Mickey shooed the rooster back to his own yard.

"Pluto!" scolded Minnie. "Chasing chickens again! Aren't you ashamed?"

Pluto *was* a bit ashamed, but only because he had let the rooster bully him. Creeping out from under the

porch, he wagged his tail and sheepishly tried to grin.

"I think it's a good thing Figaro is going to stay with you," said Minnie to Mickey.

"Figaro is a little gentleman. He can teach Pluto how to behave."

With that, Minnie handed Figaro to Mickey. Then she got into her car and drove away.

Minnie was hardly out of sight, when Figaro jumped out of Mickey's arms and scampered into the house. In the kitchen, he saw a pitcher of cream sitting on the table.

One short jump brought Figaro to the tabletop, and right to the cream. The pitcher wobbled, then tipped

 over. Cream spilled and ran off the table and onto the floor.

Pluto growled warningly as Figaro lapped up the cream.

"Take it easy, Pluto," said Mickey, cleaning up the mess. "Figaro is our guest."

When Figaro heard that, he wrinkled his nose at Pluto and stuck out his little pink tongue.

Later that day, Figaro romped through the ashes in the fireplace and left sooty footprints on the carpet.

"Figaro's a very *messy* little guest," said Ferdie as he got out the vacuum cleaner.

At dinnertime, Pluto ate his dog food, the way a good dog should. But no matter how much Mickey and the boys coaxed, Figaro wouldn't touch the special food Minnie had left for him. He did, at last, nibble on some imported sardines.

"He's a *fussy* little guest," said Morty.

At bedtime, Pluto curled up in his basket without any complaint.

However, Figaro would not use the fine, soft cushion Minnie had brought for him. Instead, he got into bed

with Morty and nipped at his toes. Then he got into bed with Ferdie and tickled both his ears. Finally, he bounced off to the kitchen, and the house became very still.

"Uncle Mickey," called Morty, "did you remember to close the kitchen window?"

"Oh, no!" cried Mickey. He jumped out of bed and ran quickly to the kitchen.

The kitchen window was half open, and

Figaro was nowhere to be seen!

"Figaro!" Mickey and the boys called. They searched through the entire house. They looked upstairs and

downstairs, under every chair, and behind every door. But they couldn't find the little kitten anywhere.

They even went out into the yard and looked under every bush and behind every tree.

But there was still no Figaro.

"He really ran away," Mickey said

at last. Morty and Ferdie followed Mickey back to the house, where Mickey put his coat on over his pajamas.

"You two stay here," he told the boys. "Pluto and I will find Figaro. Leave the porch light on for us."

Pluto didn't wag his tail, and he didn't even try to grin as he got out of his cozy basket. But off he went to help Mickey in the search.

They went to Minnie's house first, but Figaro wasn't there.

Then they went to the park down the street. "Have you seen a little black-and-white kitten?" Mickey asked the policeman at the gate.

"I certainly have!" answered the policeman. "He was by the pond, teasing the ducks!"

Mickey and Pluto hurried to the pond. Figaro wasn't there, either, but he had been. He had left behind some small, muddy footprints.

Mickey and Pluto followed the trail of footprints to Main Street, where they met some firemen.

"I'm looking for a black-and-white kitten," said Mickey.

"We just rescued a black-and-white kitten," said one of the firemen. "He had climbed a telephone pole and needed help getting down. He ran through the alley."

In the alley, a dairy truck driver was cleaning up some broken eggs.

"Have you seen a kitten?" asked Mickey.

"Have I!" cried the driver. "He knocked over my eggs!"

Mickey groaned as he paid for the broken eggs.

When Mickey and Pluto finally trudged home, it was dawn. They had searched the whole town. They had even been to the police station, but they had not found Figaro.

"What will Aunt Minnie say?" asked the boys.

"I hate to think what Aunt Minnie will say," answered poor Mickey.

Before long, Minnie drove up. Mickey and the boys looked worried as they went out to meet her.

"Where is Figaro?" asked Minnie.

No one answered.

"Something has happened to him!"

Minnie cried. "Can't I trust you to watch *just one* sweet little kitten for me?"

Just then, there was a loud clucking from the yard next door. At least a dozen frantic hens came flapping over the fence. Close behind the hens was Figaro.

"There's your sweet little kitten!" exclaimed Mickey.

"Figaro!" cried Minnie, not believing her eyes.

At the sound of her voice, Figaro skidded to a stop. He sat down, meowed gently, then quickly tried to smooth his dusty fur with his little pink tongue.

"He ran away last night," explained Mickey. "He teased the ducks in the park and broke the eggs in the

dairy truck

and—"

"And now

he's chasing

chickens!"

finished Minnie.

"I had hoped he'd teach Pluto some manners," Minnie went on. "Instead, Pluto has been teaching him to do those naughty things. Teasing ducks! Chasing chickens! The very idea! I'll never leave him here again."

"It wasn't Pluto's fault!" protested Morty.

"Pluto didn't
do anything bad,"
added Ferdie. "He
stayed up all
night, trying to
find Figaro."

But Minnie

wouldn't listen. She picked up Figaro, got into her car,

and drove quickly away.

"Don't worry, boys," said Mickey. "We'll tell her the

whole story later, when she's not so upset."

"Please don't tell her too soon," begged Morty. "As long as Aunt Minnie thinks Pluto is a bad dog, we won't have to kitten-sit Figaro."

Mickey smiled and said, "Maybe we *should* wait a little while. We could all use some peace and quiet. And we did learn one thing: there's not much sitting in kitten-sitting."

Walt Disney's
Donald Duck
and the
Buried Treasure

One afternoon, Donald Duck and his nephews, Huey, Dewey, and Louie, were taking a drive. They found themselves going through a small village near the water. The nephews wanted to watch the boats sail in and out of the harbor. Just as they were about to ask their uncle if they could get a closer look at the boats, Donald suddenly jammed on the brakes.

"What's wrong, Unca Donald?" asked his nephews.

Donald pointed to a sign on a shop. It said FISHING SUPPLIES. In the shop's window, another sign read GENUINE PIRATE MAPS 25¢.

"Pirate treasure!" the boys yelled. "Yippee! Can we get a map, Unca Donald? Please!"

"Of course," Donald said with a big smile.

Donald went inside the shop and found the shopkeeper.

"Are you looking for a treasure map?" the shopkeeper asked slyly.

Donald nodded his head, and the man handed him a rolled-up map.

"Cheap enough," Donald said as he gave the man a quarter.

Then, because treasure hunters need things besides maps, he sold Donald a shovel, a pickax, a compass, ropes for hauling up the treasure, and sacks for carrying it home. Last of all, he rented Donald a boat—the biggest one at the dock.

Closely

following the

treasure map,

Donald and

his nephews

soon found

themselves

rowing out to an island. Donald dropped the anchor,

and they all hopped out of the boat.

"Here we are!" Donald cried. "Treasure Island!"

"Yippee!" his nephews yelled.

Donald and his nephews tied up the boat and stepped out onto the island. Then Donald read the directions on the map: "Look for the forked tree. Take ten paces north. Then dig."

Donald and his nephews looked around for the tree.

"There it is!" Dewey yelled excitedly. "Let's go."

As soon as they reached the tree, they began digging a hole ten paces to the north. But there was no treasure. So they dug some more: ten paces to the west, and one more to the east. They dug the holes deep, and they dug the holes wide.

But there was no treasure to be found.

Donald was furious. He threw down his shovel and glared at the treasure map. "This map is a fake!" he shouted. "There is no treasure buried on this island. Phooey!"

"Shh!" his nephews whispered. "Don't shout, Unca Donald. You'll scare the ghost away."

Donald blinked. "What ghost?" he asked.

"It must be the ghost of Captain Kidd," they said. "Listen!"

Then Donald heard it, too.

Clank, clank, clank, clank.

"T-there's no such thing as a ghost," Donald said in a quavering voice.

But his nephews weren't so sure. They convinced Donald to see where the noise was coming from. Slowly, they crept up a hill, following the noise.

They looked down and saw people digging all over the island. Each had a "real" pirate treasure map!

"I knew it!" Donald yelled. "These maps are fakes! Okay, boys. The joke's on us. Anyway, we had fun digging. Let's go now."

They found their way back to the boat. Donald started to pull up the anchor. He tugged and tugged, but he couldn't budge it!

"Give me a hand, boys!" cried Donald.

They all pulled together. Finally, the anchor did come up—bringing a big iron sea chest with it.

Donald lifted his pickax. "Stand back, kids!" he cried.

At the first crack, the old lock on the chest snapped.

Donald lifted the lid slowly. Everybody gasped. Then

everybody shouted. Inside were hundreds and hundreds

of gold and silver coins.

"We found it!" the nephews shouted. "It's real pirate treasure! Yippee!"

"I knew we would find it!" exclaimed Donald.

They couldn't wait to go home and count all their coins,

so they

quickly

rowed

back

to the

mainland and carried the chest to their car.

"Just one second, boys," Donald said, winking. Donald

GENUINE PIRATE MAPS 25¢

had something to take care of before they could go home. He walked back to the shop.

The shop owner was grinning. "Well, how was the treasure hunt?" he asked.

Donald dropped a pirate coin in the shopkeeper's hand. "Not bad," he said.

The man's eyes bulged as he stared at the gold coin.

"Thanks for the map," Donald said as he waved good-bye and walked out the door.

Then Donald waited outside. In a second, the shop door flew open and the man came running out. In one hand he held a shovel, in the other a map. "They really are genuine!" he cried.

Donald and his nephews watched the shopkeeper hop into his boat.

"Good luck!" Donald yelled.

"Happy hunting!" cried Huey, Dewey, and Louie.

They all waved good-bye,

and then they drove home

to count their genuine

pirate treasure.

Walt Disney's
The Bravest Dog

It was a sunny day and Minnie Mouse lay sunbathing in Mickey Mouse's backyard. Pluto was resting peacefully beside her. Suddenly, Minnie and Pluto

jumped up as they saw Mickey running out of the house toward his car.

"Mickey, where are you going?" asked Minnie.

"There's been trouble, Minnic!" Mickey cried. "A circus train was going through town, and some of the animals got loose. The sheriff called and asked me to help find them before they start to cause trouble."

Pluto wanted to be a wild-animal hunter, too. So he put his front paws on the car door, begging to go along.

But Mickey quickly shook his head. "Not this time, Pluto," he said. "You stay here with Minnie."

Then Mickey
started his
car and
drove
through
the gate
and down
the road.

"Woof!" Pluto sneezed in the cloud of dust. Why
did he always have to stay at home? Why couldn't
he be a wild-animal hunter like Mickey?

Then Pluto had a great idea. He tugged at Minnie's skirt, looked at her pleadingly, and pointed his paw toward the road.

Minnie smiled. She knew exactly what Pluto wanted to do. "Well, all right," she said. "I don't think it's likely any of the animals have come this far. And I feel like taking a walk, anyway. It's such a nice day."

Joyously, Pluto led the way down the path toward the river. He was a hunter after all.

After walking for a while, Minnie and Pluto
entered a meadow. They soon heard a sharp hissing
sound coming from the grass.

"Eeeek! Snakes! They must have escaped from
the circus train!" Minnie cried. She was not very

fond of snakes. In fact, she was quite scared of them.

Pluto wasn't very fond of snakes, either. Soon his

teeth began to chatter. Then his tail curled up in a knot.

But he had to be brave. He was a hunter, after all. He

pushed through the tall grass and saw . . .

. . . a small orange cat! Her back was arched, and she hissed fiercely at Pluto. Behind her lay six kittens, curled up in a cozy bed of moss.

"Oh—oh, my!" Minnie said with a chuckle. "And we thought that harmless little cat was a snake. Come on, Pluto, we mustn't disturb her."

Now Minnie and Pluto stayed close together. If

there *were* any circus snakes around, they didn't want to run into them!

"It would be fun to find a bear cub, though," said Minnie. "Or a

seal! I love seals. I wonder if a seal could come this far."

As if in answer, they heard a splash coming from the river ahead. They also heard some sharp little barks.

Minnie and Pluto looked toward the river with surprise. Could there really be a seal there?

Pluto had to find out. Seals barked sometimes. Maybe this was finally his chance to catch a wild animal!

Quickly, Pluto ran toward the river. When he got

there, he dashed down the pier and plunged into the cold water.

Right behind him was Minnie. "Be careful, Pluto!" she cried.

As Pluto got closer, he realized that it wasn't a seal splashing around in the water. It was a whimpering, little puppy.

As soon as Minnie realized what Pluto had found, she said, "Get him, Pluto! Bring him in."

Pluto did as he was told and laid the puppy at Minnie's feet a minute later.

"A cat and a puppy!" Minnie laughed. "We'd better not tell anybody about our wild-animal hunting!"

She petted the shivering puppy until it was dry. Then the little fellow raced off up the path.

"Come on, Pluto," Minnie said as she patted his head. "I love you even if you never capture anything wilder than a puppy dog."

Silently, they continued on. Poor Pluto's tail was tucked between his legs, and his long ears drooped sadly. He had really wanted to capture one of the circus animals, and now he might never have the chance.

"Let's go back to the house," Minnie suggested. "I think a big bone is just what you need."

Back at
Mickey's
house, Minnie
went directly
to the kitchen.
She opened
the kitchen
door, but then
stopped. Milk

was spattered across the floor, pieces of broken dishes

lay on the floor, a chair was overturned, and one window

was half open, the curtain blowing in the fresh summer breeze.

"Oh, Pluto!" Minnie exclaimed. "Somebody has been in here! Maybe it's one of the circus animals. It could still be hiding around here! What should we do?"

Pluto snarled bravely and began sniffing around the kitchen for a trail. This was finally his chance to be a wild-animal hunter.

"Be careful," Minnie said. "It may be very fierce!"

Pluto barked loudly. Then he leaped through the open window and raced across the yard to the woodshed.

Just then, Mickey drove up. "We caught the animals," he called. "All except—"

Minnie ran over to Mickey and put her finger to her lips. She pointed at the shed where Pluto was slowly nosing through the door. He had stopped barking, and there was a terrible quiet as he disappeared inside the shed.

Minnie held her breath.

Then, very, very slowly, Pluto came out, his tail wagging proudly as he walked toward his friends.

Mickey gasped, then started to laugh. Minnie laughed, too, hardly able to believe her eyes.

For there, on Pluto's back, sat a tiny little monkey, wearing a brightly colored red circus ruffle around his neck.

"Pluto, you did it!" Mickey exclaimed. "You

captured the only wild animal we couldn't find. Well, maybe he's not so *very* wild," he added, as the little monkey jumped into his arms. "But it took a lot of courage to go into the woodshed after him!"

"Pluto *thinks* brave," Minnie said proudly. "He's been a brave dog all afternoon."

Tired from his busy day, Pluto lay down on the grass

Walt Disney's
HAPPY SAILING,
MICKEY MOUSE

One lovely summer day, Mickey Mouse asked his girlfriend, Minnie, if she'd like to take a rowboat ride.

"I'd love to go on a nice, easy boat ride," Minnie said with a smile. "This will be fun."

Just then, Goofy came running by. "Hey, Mickey!" he shouted. "It's the perfect day for a

run. Do you want to come join me?"

"No, thanks," said Mickey. "Today, Minnie and I are going for a nice, easy boat ride."

"Okay," called Goofy. "Have a good time."

Then Mickey and Minnie climbed into the boat and began to row away. As Goofy started running again, a pesky squirrel crossed his path. Goofy didn't see it and stepped on its tail.

The squirrel leaped away and landed in the boat, right on Mickey's lap. Mickey was so startled that he jumped up. This startled Minnie, and she jumped up, too. All of the commotion caused the

boat to wobble. It wobbled so much that it tipped over, sending Mickey and Minnie into the water.

Luckily, Donald Duck was nearby, in his speed-boat, and saw what had happened.

"Don't worry! I'll rescue you!" he called. Once they were onboard, he said, "Why don't you folks ride in my boat for a while? You can take it easy and let the engine do the work."

"Thanks!" said Mickey. He and Minnie sat back and relaxed, listening to the happy *putt-putt* of the engine. Maybe we can still have a nice, easy boat ride, thought Mickey.

But when the boat reached the middle of the lake, the engine suddenly stopped!

"Oh, no!" Mickey groaned. They were now stuck in the middle of the lake and they didn't have any oars.

"What should we do?" asked Minnie.

"Wait, I have an idea!" cried Donald Duck. He took off his hat and started to paddle with it. Luckily for them, Minnie and Mickey were both wearing hats, too. Huffing and puffing, they paddled their way back to shore.

Finally, they were back on land, and the last thing

 Mickey wanted to do was to get back into the water. "Let's just sit on these nice, comfortable beach chairs," he suggested to Minnie. "We can't get into trouble sitting over here."

So, Mickey and Minnie relaxed in the sun for a few hours, enjoying being dry for a change. And since it was time for lunch, they bought two hot dogs.

As they were enjoying their lunch, Pluto came running by. He was hungry, too. And when he saw the two delicious hot dogs, he decided that he wanted one. So, he

jumped onto Mickey's lap and tried to grab the food.

"Stop it, boy!" cried Mickey.

"Pluto," said Minnie, "if you want a hot dog, we can get you one."

But it was too late. . . .

Pluto knocked Mickey and Minnie right into the water!

"Here we are, wet all over again," Mickey said, as he and Minnie swam back to shore.

"I don't know what's going on," said Minnie. "We just can't seem to stay dry today!"

When they got back to land, Mickey and Minnie warmed themselves in the sun.

Soon, Donald Duck's nephews, Huey, Dewey, and Louie, sailed by in their sailboat.

"Hey, Mickey," called Dewey. "Would you and

Minnie like

to borrow

our boat

and go

sailing?

There's a

good wind

today."

"I've always wanted to go sailing," said Minnie excitedly. "Sailing is supposed to be a lot of fun."

"All right," agreed Mickey. "I guess I can give boating just one more chance."

So, Mickey and Minnie hopped into the nephews' boat and took off.

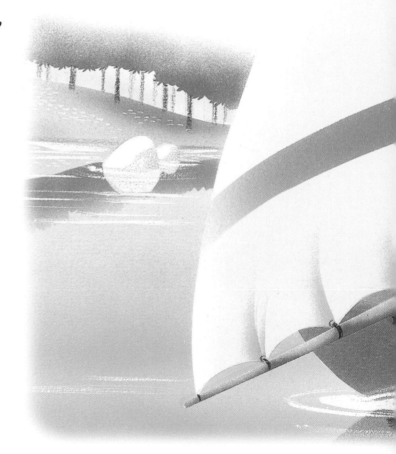

"Ah, this is the life," said Mickey. It *was* the perfect day for a sail.

"Yes, a nice, easy boat ride," said Minnie. "It's really about time."

But suddenly, the wind stopped blowing!

And then the boat stopped moving.

"Oh, no!" Mickey groaned. "We're stranded again!"

Mickey and Minnie tried to paddle with their hands,

but it was no use. They kept going around in circles.

"What are we going to do?" Mickey wondered. The two of them tried to come up with a new plan, but they couldn't think of anything. Suddenly, Mickey looked

up. He saw Goofy and Donald Duck, each in their own

rowboat, coming toward them.

"We thought you might need some help," said

Donald.

"Oh, thank
you for rescuing
us!" cried Minnie.

"After all,
that's what
friends are for,"
said Goofy.

The sun began to set over the peaceful lake. Mickey and Minnie sat back happily as they *finally* got their nice, easy boat ride.

WALT DISNEP's

MICKEY MOUSE
and the
Great Lot Plot

THIS
LAND
FOR
SALE!

"Look at that!" Morty cried as he and Ferdie dropped their baseball and their bat, and stared at the sign in front of them: THIS LAND FOR SALE!

"I can't believe it!" cried Minnie Mouse. "This is the

only vacant lot left for blocks around."

"Maybe whoever buys the land will let children play here," Mickey Mouse said hopefully.

"I'm going to buy it," said a voice behind them. It was Uncle Scrooge McDuck. "It's right next to my money bin, and it's the best place for my new business—Scrooge's Perfectly Planted, Picked, and Processed

Patented Pickled Preserves!" Morty and Ferdie wrinkled their noses.

"Ugh! How can anyone think pickled preserves are more important than baseball?" they cried.

But Scrooge certainly thought so. "Scrooge's Perfectly Planted, Picked, and Processed Patented Pickled Preserves will be a good business," he said. Then he turned and walked away to his money bin.

Mickey and the others followed. They found Scrooge

seated on a big pile of money, happily counting it.

"Won't you please think this over, Uncle Scrooge?" Mickey asked. "The children really need a place to run and play, and this lot is perfect."

"No!" answered Uncle Scrooge. "My mind is made up, and that's final!"

"But playgrounds are important!" insisted Mickey. Then, before he quite knew what he was saying, he made

an announcement of his own. "I'm going to buy the lot, and I'll make it into a playground for everyone to enjoy."

Scrooge laughed so hard, he rolled off the pile of money. "There's no way you will get the money to buy this lot," said Scrooge, still laughing.

As they left the money bin, Mickey's brave smile
changed
to a frown.
"Where will
I get the
money?"
he asked.
But

Minnie and the boys were bubbling with excitement.
"Why, we will earn it!" they exclaimed. "Don't worry,
Mickey. Our friends will be happy to help, too!"

And so they were! Those next few weeks, Mickey's friends were the busiest people in town. Busiest of all was Mickey himself.

He helped Donald Duck and his nephews wash cars. (Then he helped dry Huey, Dewey, and Louie, who got as wet as the cars they were washing.)

He helped Goofy, whose dog-walking job became

too much

for him to

handle

alone.

And he

helped Morty and Ferdie sell the pies and cakes that

Minnie

and Daisy

Duck

baked.

At the end of the month, Mickey counted up all the money that everyone had earned and given to him. It

came to exactly five hundred dollars. That wasn't very much, and Mickey was worried!

The next day, he went to see Uncle Scrooge. "I'm very sad," he said. "All together, we've only been able to earn five hundred dollars, Uncle Scrooge, and I know that isn't enough money to buy the lot. You certainly can pay much more than that for it!"

"Too bad, Mickey," Uncle Scrooge said, smiling. "Looks like the lot will be mine. It sure is a perfect place for my new pickled preserves factory."

Later that day, Scrooge walked happily down the street and stopped in front of the empty lot.

"Hi, Uncle Scrooge!" cried Morty and Ferdie. "Got

any jobs you want done?"

"Certainly not!" snapped Uncle Scrooge. "The only help I need is in understanding what's so important about a playground. A lot of foolishness, if you ask me. Humph!"

"We can't tell you," said Morty.

"But we can show you," added Ferdie. "Here, catch!"

And before he knew it, Uncle Scrooge was out on the empty lot, playing a fast game of baseball.

It was nearly dark when the three finally sat down to rest.

"Well, Uncle Scrooge," said Morty, "now do you see what's so great about a playground?"

Uncle Scrooge was puffing so hard, he couldn't even answer Morty.

The next day, the boys were waiting when Uncle Scrooge came down the street.

"Tag!" shouted Morty.

"You're It!" yelled Ferdie.

And before he knew what had happened, Uncle Scrooge was chasing the boys across the field.

"You can play all kinds of good games on a play-ground," said Morty when they stopped to rest at last.

"Humph!" said Uncle Scrooge. This time, he was so tired that he fell asleep right there under a tree. While he slept, he had a very strange dream. It was like no dream Uncle Scrooge had ever had before.

The next day, Mickey and his friends watched as the owner of the land put up a new sign on the lot. It said:

SOLD TO SCROOGE McDUCK.

Everyone groaned—everyone, that is, except Scrooge. He was overjoyed.

As they all turned to leave, their faces sad, Scrooge shouted, "Wait here a few minutes. I have a surprise for you all!"

Soon, workmen began to arrive. They lifted swings and slides into place! They started to dig a swimming pool! In the corner, they marked the lines for a baseball diamond!

Scrooge just stood there and grinned, while Mickey, his nephews, and Goofy gave three tremendous cheers.

"Uncle Scrooge," Mickey said, "how can we ever thank you enough? We're awfully glad you changed your mind! Now we can buy *uniforms* for all the baseball teams, using our five hundred dollars!"

The day of the first game in the new park finally arrived. Uncle Scrooge was given the honor of hitting the very first ball.

"Hurrah!" the crowd cheered as the ball soared into the air.

The cheer was cut short by the sound of breaking glass. The ball had crashed through a window in Scrooge's own money bin!

"Uh-oh! Sorry about your window, Uncle Scrooge," called Mickey.

But Uncle Scrooge was already on his way to first base. "It's only glass," he shouted over his shoulder. "But did you see that? I do believe I hit a home run!"

Walt Disney's
Donald Duck's
Christmas Tree

It was the day before Christmas, and Donald Duck was busy getting ready. He was just about finished wrapping all of his gifts. The last thing he had to do was to go get a Christmas tree.

Donald put on his coat, cap, and mittens. He also picked up his shiny ax.

"Come along," he called to Pluto, who was visiting with Donald because Mickey Mouse was away for the holidays. "We're going to the woods to find our Christmas tree."

Pluto, excited to be outside in the snow, came running out of the house and followed Donald to the woods.

Now, deep in the woods in a sturdy fir tree lived two merry chipmunks named Chip 'n' Dale.

Chip 'n' Dale were getting ready for Christmas, too.

They had found a tiny fir tree standing near their home. They were trimming it with berries and chains of dry grass when

Donald and Pluto came along.

When the chipmunks saw Donald, with Pluto prancing by his side, they left their tiny fir tree and scampered home to safety. Or, at least, they thought they were safe.

When Donald took one look at Chip 'n' Dale's sturdy

home, he said,

"This is just

the tree for

us! It will fit

perfectly in

my living

room."

Chop, chop,

chop went Donald's shiny ax. Poor Chip 'n' Dale didn't

know what to do.

"Come on, Pluto," called Donald when the tree was down. "Let's take our tree home."

So, through the woods went Donald Duck, whistling as he tramped along, dragging the fir tree home.

And among the branches sat Chip 'n' Dale, enjoying the nice ride.

When Donald got home, he set his tree in the corner next to the window.

"There," he said when he was through. "Now, it's time to trim the tree." Donald went up to the attic and brought out boxes of festive ornaments and lights.

Donald Duck had no idea, but from their hiding place up in the branches, Chip 'n' Dale looked on as he decorated the tree. They watched as Donald looped long strings of colorful lights over the branches of the tree.

They saw Donald hang brightly colored ornaments
all over the
tree. They
even watched
Pluto as he
helped with
the garland.
"There!"
cried Donald

as he hung the last ornament. "Doesn't that look fine?"

"Bowwow!" Pluto barked in agreement.

And indeed it was a beautiful Christmas tree.

"Now, I'll get everybody's presents so that we can pile them under the tree," said Donald. "Pluto, you stay here. I'll be right back."

Pluto sat down by the tree, admiring it.

As soon as Donald was out of sight, Chip 'n' Dale decided that it was time to have some Christmas fun of their own.

They danced up and down the branches of the tree until the needles quivered.

They raced around the colorful lights. And they made silly faces at themselves in the shiny colored balls.

Then they laughed and laughed until their little sides shook.

"Grrr," growled Pluto disapprovingly.

But Chip 'n' Dale didn't care what Pluto thought.
Chip picked off some of the shiny ornaments and
started throwing them at Pluto!

"Grrr!" Pluto
growled again.

Then Dale
picked an
ornament off the
tree and threw it
at Pluto, too!

Pluto jumped and barely caught it in his teeth. Just then, in walked Donald Duck with an armful of presents.

"Pluto!" he cried. "Stop it!" He thought Pluto had been snatching the ornaments from the tree.

Poor Pluto! There was no sign of Chip 'n' Dale anywhere.

"Now, be good," said Donald, "while I bring in the rest of the presents."

No sooner had Donald gone than Chip 'n' Dale appeared once more.

Plunk! Chip put a cracked plastic ornament over his head. Dale laughed and laughed.

But Pluto did not think it was funny at all. They were spoiling Donald's tree!

"Grrr!" he growled, getting ready to jump.

"Pluto!" cried Donald Duck from the doorway. "What's wrong with you? Do you want to ruin the tree?"

Of course, Chip 'n' Dale were safely out of sight. And poor Pluto could not explain.

"Now, you'll just have to go outside and stay in the yard for the rest of Christmas Eve," Donald said

sternly to Pluto.

But just then, up in the treetop, Chip grew tired of wearing the Christmas

ornament. He pulled it off and let it drop.

Crash! It bounced off the floor.

"What was that?" cried Donald.

"Bowwow!" said Pluto, pointing to the tree.

Then Dale began to play with the colored lights, twisting them so they turned on and off.

"What's going on?" cried Donald Duck.

"Bowwow! Bowwow!" said Pluto, pointing to the

tree again.

Donald peered among

the branches until he

spied Chip 'n' Dale.

"Well, well," he

said with a chuckle as he

lifted them down. "So

you're the mischief-makers. And to think I blamed poor

Pluto. I'm sorry, Pluto," said Donald.

Pluto marched over to the door and held it open. He thought Chip 'n' Dale should go back home.

"Oh, Pluto!" cried Donald. "It's Christmas Eve. We must be kind to everyone, even pesky chipmunks. The spirit of Christmas is love, you know."

So, Pluto made friends with Chip 'n' Dale.

And when Donald's friends came by to sing carols, eat cookies, and drink eggnog, they all agreed this was by far their happiest Christmas Eve ever.

It was a perfect day for a cookout, and Mickey Mouse and his nephews, Morty and Ferdie, were in Mickey's backyard, getting ready to make lunch. Mickey was putting charcoal in the grill, while Morty brought out the food.

"I wonder what's taking Minnie so long," said Mickey. "She's never late."

"I hope she remembers the fudge layer cake she promised," said Ferdie.

A few minutes later, Pluto barked a friendly welcome to Minnie as she came hurrying through the gate.

"I'm sorry to be late," she said, handing the boys her cake. "But I have great news. I've just been elected chairperson of the Charity Pet Show."

"With you in charge, it's certain to be a success," Mickey said enthusiastically.

"Why, thank you," Minnie said. "I certainly hope so. We have to raise a lot of money to build a brand-new shelter for stray animals."

"We should enter Pluto in the show!" Morty suggested excitedly.

"But Pluto isn't a show dog," Mickey reminded the boys.

"We can train him and teach him to do tricks!" said Ferdie. "Can't we? Please."

"All right," Mickey said, "but only because it will help raise money to build a shelter for stray animals."

Minnie and Mickey watched as the boys started to train Pluto for the pet show.

"Roll over, Pluto!" ordered Morty.

But Pluto didn't understand. He just sat up and wagged his tail.

"Maybe we should *show* him what we want him to do," said Ferdie.

Pluto watched, puzzled, as both boys rolled over in the grass. He still didn't understand.

"Let's try something that he *likes* to do," suggested Morty.

"That's a good idea," said Ferdie.

Then he ordered Pluto to lie down.

Instead, Pluto jumped up and began chasing his tail.

"Look, Minnie!" cried Mickey. "The boys have really got him doing tricks!"

"But they're just not the *right* tricks," wailed Morty and Ferdie.

All week
long, Morty
and Ferdie
worked
hard, trying
to teach
Pluto new

tricks. He fetched, rolled over, sat up, lay down, and

shook hands . . . but only when *he* wanted to.

Everyone was very discouraged.

"He will never win first prize," said Morty sadly.

On the day of the show, Mickey and the boys took Pluto to the empty lot next door, where the show was being held. Minnie sold Mickey three tickets, then pointed happily to the cashbox.

"We've got enough money right now to pay for the new animal shelter!" she told him.

"Hooray!" cheered the boys.

"That's great!" cried Mickey.

What *wasn't* so great was Pluto's performance

that day.

He
shook
hands when
he was told
to sit. He
rolled over
when he

should have jumped. He barked when he was supposed

to lie down. The audience roared with laughter.

Worst of all, when Police Chief O'Hara was choosing the Best Pet of the Day, Pluto growled at him! The chief didn't know it, but he was standing on the very spot where Pluto had buried a good bone!

Suddenly, screams were heard from the ticket booth.

"Help! Stop, thief! Help!"

"That's Minnie!" Mickey gasped.

"The ticket money!" yelped the boys.

Mickey, the boys, and Chief O'Hara ran to the booth.

Pluto was already at the scene of the crime when the others got there. He was busily sniffing around the booth.

"I'm all right, Mickey," Minnie said, "but all the money is gone. When I came back to get it, I saw someone running away with the cashbox."

"What did the robber look like?" asked the chief.

"I don't know," Minnie replied. "I didn't see his face."

"Which way did he go?" Mickey asked.

Just then, before Minnie could answer, Pluto took off for the woods. "He's tracking the thief!" shouted Mickey. "Go, Pluto! Stop the thief!"

"It's more likely that he's tracking a kitten," snorted Chief O'Hara.

But it was no kitten that ran screaming out of the woods. It was the thief—hanging on to the cashbox— followed by Pluto, who was clenching his teeth on the thief's suspenders!

"Save me!" yelled the thief.

S-s-snap! The thief's suspenders broke and shot him

right into the arms of Chief O'Hara.

Later that afternoon, at police headquarters, Chief O'Hara presented Pluto with the Four-Footed Hero Medal.

The chief smiled and said, "Thanks to Pluto, animals who are lost will now have a new shelter and a chance to find good homes."

Pluto proudly accepted the medal, and everyone cheered and clapped for him.

On the way back to Mickey's house, Morty grandly announced, "Pluto's better than a show dog. He's our *hero* dog."

Suddenly, Pluto barked sharply at Ferdie, who was about to cross the street.

"Ferdie! Watch out!" shouted Mickey, pulling him back to the curb. "Didn't you see that car?"

"Pluto did," said Minnie, patting him.

As soon as the street was clear of cars, they began to cross. Suddenly, they saw an old man drop his cane.

With a friendly wag of his tail, Pluto picked up the cane and gave it back to him.

"That's a nice dog you have," the old man said to Mickey, and they all watched, smiling, as Pluto bounded on ahead.

When they got to Mickey's house, Pluto was waiting on the doorstep.
He wagged his tail and barked his friendly welcome.

"Do you know what, boys?" said Mickey happily. "Who cares whether Pluto wins prizes or is a hero? He's everybody's friend—and that's what counts!"

Minnie, Morty, and Ferdie agreed. Then, without being told, Pluto shook hands with everyone because *this* was a time when *he* wanted to!

Walt Disney's COWBOY MICKEY

ickey Mouse was busily packing his suitcase.

"Hurry up," urged Minnie. "I just can't wait to get to the Lucky Star Dude Ranch!"

"I'm excited, too!" Mickey told her. "I've always wanted to learn how to ride a horse."

"And I've always wanted to be a cowgirl," Minnie said happily.

Just then, Goofy raced into Mickey's house with his suitcase. "I'm all packed and ready to go!" he shouted. "I'm going to learn how to ride a horse and twirl a lasso so I can perform in the Lucky Star Rodeo."

"Is there really going to be a rodeo at the

ranch?" asked

Minnie.

"That's what

I heard," said

Mickey.

"Wouldn't it

be great if we

could all take

part in it?"

"Yes," agreed Minnie. "Let's try our best to learn as

much as possible so we can all be in the rodeo."

Goofy couldn't wait to show everyone how well he could ride. The minute he reached the Lucky Star Dude Ranch, he hopped on the first horse he saw. But he jumped on it backward!

"Uh-oh!" Goofy gulped. "What do I do now?" He held on tightly to the horse's tail as it bucked around in circles.

Luckily, Minnie had brought a bunch of carrots with her to feed the horses. She held them out to the horse, and he  stopped jumping and whinnied happily as he trotted over to eat them. Goofy quickly jumped off the horse.

"Whew! That was really close," he gasped. "Minnie, thanks a lot for showing up with those carrots."

"It looks like you folks need a few riding lessons," said the owner of the ranch as he walked over to them. "Call me Cowboy Bob, and let me show you the right way to get on a horse."

He held the horses' reins as he helped Mickey, Minnie, and Goofy step up and onto their horses.

Cowboy Bob then showed them all the proper way to ride a horse.

"Hey, this isn't hard at all," bragged Goofy as he trotted along on his horse. "Now I'm ready to learn how to use a lasso."

"Lassoing takes lots of practice," said Cowboy Bob. Then he gave Goofy his first lasso lesson.

That night, Mickey and Minnie and some of the ranch hands had a cookout under the stars.

"Yippee-ti-yi-yo!" they all sang around the campfire.

Suddenly, they heard a wild cry and saw a strange shadow.

"I think it's a coyote!" whispered Mickey.

Quickly,

Cowboy Bob shone

his flashlight at

the shadow.

"It's not a

coyote—it's

Goofy!" said

Minnie with a

giggle. "He's trying to trick us by walking on his hands!"

"I fooled you, didn't I?" said Goofy, who couldn't

stop laughing at his silly trick.

The next day, Mickey and Minnie practiced their
riding while Goofy practiced with his lasso.

"You're learning very fast," Cowboy Bob said to Mickey
and Minnie. "I bet you'll both be good enough to
perform in the rodeo."

"How about me?" asked Goofy. "Watch how well

I twirl this lasso." Goofy whirled the lasso and got his foot caught in the rope.

"Whoops!" he cried. "I'd better practice some more."

So, while Minnie and Mickey galloped all around the ranch, Goofy practiced with his lasso. He tried to rope fences and he tried to rope the Lucky Star sign, but he always ended up roping himself.

Finally, the day of the big rodeo arrived. Cowboy Bob had great news. He said that everyone staying at the Lucky Star Dude Ranch could perform in the rodeo. That meant Minnie, Mickey, and Goofy could all be in the show together.

"Let's all line up for the grand rodeo parade!"

shouted

Cowboy Bob.

"Where's

Mickey?" asked

Minnie. "I

haven't seen

him anywhere."

"I don't

know," said

Cowboy Bob. "I haven't seen him, either."

At that very moment, Mickey was asleep! He'd

forgotten to set his alarm clock to wake up in time for the rodeo. But as the noisy crowd passed by his window, he woke up. When Mickey realized how late he'd slept, he knew he had to hurry or he'd miss all the fun.

Mickey got dressed quickly and dashed out the door. I'd better take all the shortcuts I can, he thought, as he raced across a field and jumped over a fence.

"Uh-oh," Mickey groaned. "I think maybe I shouldn't have jumped over that fence." He had just landed on a bucking bronco in the middle of the rodeo arena!

Everyone cheered as Mickey held tightly to the reins, riding the bronco. "This is sort of fun!" he cried as he waved his hat to the crowd.

"Ladies and gentlemen," called the rodeo announcer,

"Mickey Mouse just broke the ranch record for the longest time riding a bronco."

The crowd cheered again.

When Mickey
jumped off the
bronco, it began to
chase him. "What
do I do now?"
shouted Mickey.

"I'll lasso him for
you," yelled Goofy, but he lassoed Mickey instead.

However, seeing Mickey all roped up was so funny,
even the bucking bronco stopped for a chuckle.

Then, Mickey quickly untied himself and raced away.

Later that day, everybody cheered as Cowboy Bob presented the rodeo ribbons.

Minnie won for being the best cowgirl and taking good care of the horses.

Mickey won for his bronco riding.

And Goofy won for trying to lasso anything and everything in sight!

That night, everyone sat around the campfire one last time. "This has been the most fun I've ever had," Mickey told Minnie.

"Me, too," she said with a sigh. "I love being a cowgirl."

Just then, they all saw an odd profile against the full moon.

"I'll bet it's Goofy joking again," said Mickey.

"Nope! I'm right here," said Goofy.

"Look, it's a real coyote!" shouted Mickey. "Now, I truly feel like a cowboy."

"Do you want me to lasso him?" asked Goofy.

"No, thanks!" everyone said with a laugh.

Beautifully illustrated volumes filled with magical Disney stories

0-7868-3402-1

0-7868-3359-9

0-7868-3234-7

0-7868-3247-9

Collections for every family to treasure!

$15.99 each!
($19.99 CAN)

Collect Them All!

0-7868-3260-6

0-7868-3444-7

0-7868-3487-0

0-7868-3290-8

0-7868-3379-3

0-7868-3342-4

© Disney

Disney PRESS

Visit us at
www.disneybooks.com

Available at
bookstores and
retailers everywhere